For: Maisey

First published in 2015 by
Rockpool Children's Books Ltd.

This edition published in 2015 by Rockpool Children's
Books Ltd. in association with Albury Books.
Albury Court, Albury, Thame
OX9 2LP, United Kingdom

Printed in Turkey

ISBN 978-1-906081-81-2 (Paperback)

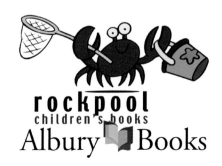

rockpool
children's books
Albury Books

Sam Walshaw

Minnie
the Minnow

Minnie Minnow was feeling
very sad and lonely.
Minnie had no friends
because she was
so different.

All the other fish
had lovely bright colours,
they all had friends,
except for Minnie.
No one ever talked to Minnie.

She was just grey and dull!

Being the odd one out
Minnie had no friends,
so she decided she would go
and find one!

The ocean was a big place,
there must be someone
who would be her friend?

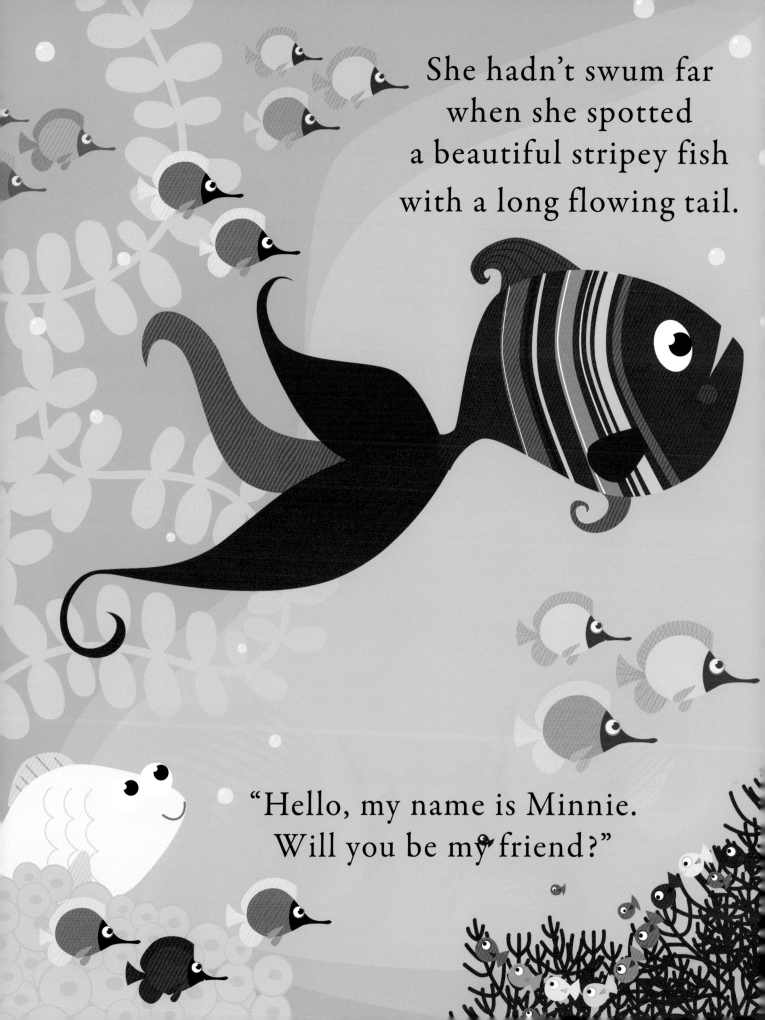

She hadn't swum far
when she spotted
a beautiful stripey fish
with a long flowing tail.

"Hello, my name is Minnie.
Will you be my friend?"

"Oh, I couldn't possibly be your friend,
you're far too dull and grey!"

"Oh, ok", said Minnie with a sniffle
and off she swam.

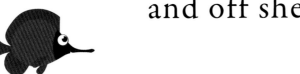

Swimming amongst the coral,
Minnie spotted a lovely green
patterned fish!
"Hello, my name is Minnie,
will you be my friend?"

"Hmmm...I really couldn't be friends with you.
You are far too dull and grey!"

"Ok", said Minnie,
fighting back the tears, and off she swam.

Just past the old anchor,
Minnie spotted a very handsome
spotty fish!

"Hello, my name
is Minnie,
will you be
my friend?"

"Most certainly not. No. Not at all. You're far too dull and grey!"

"Oh, ok", said a very sad Minnie as her eyes filled with tears.

Down by the wreck,
Minnie saw shark,
who also looked very sad.

"What's wrong?"
asked Minnie,
"You look sad too.
Will no one
be your friend either?"

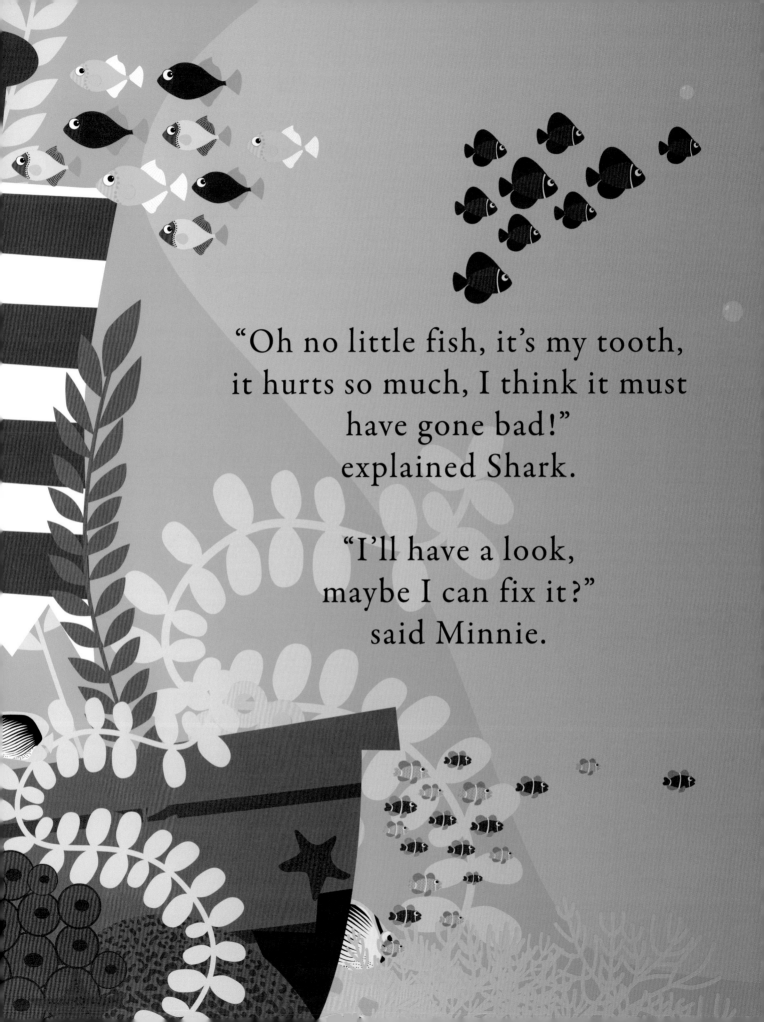

"Oh no little fish, it's my tooth,
it hurts so much, I think it must
have gone bad!"
explained Shark.

"I'll have a look,
maybe I can fix it?"
said Minnie.

Shark opened his huge mouth,
and in swam Minnie, past
the rows of sharp pointy teeth!

"Oh yes, I see,
it's just a tin can
stuck between your teeth.
I can soon fix that", she said,
reassuring Shark.

With a bit of a huff,
and a lot of puff,
Minnie dislodged the can.
" Thank you little fish,
that feels
much better now.
You are so clever!"

When Minnie came out of Sharks mouth,
she was met by a big group of fish.
"Wow Minnie, how did you do that?"
they chorused.

"How do you glow in the
dark like that? It's amazing!"

"I glow in the dark?
Really? Wow!"
said a surprised
Minnie.

Minnie's special talent made her very useful.

She helped spotty fish's little fish, who were scared of the dark, to get to sleep!

With her shining light she helped the fish with the flowing tail to find things!

Minnie helped fancy fish find her way home
through a deep dark trench!

She even agreed to
sit inside
stripey fish's
pumpkin on
Halloween night.

Minnie was a busy little fish now,
she had many friends, and no one
called her dull and grey

...ever again!

Enjoy another Minnie book in the series!

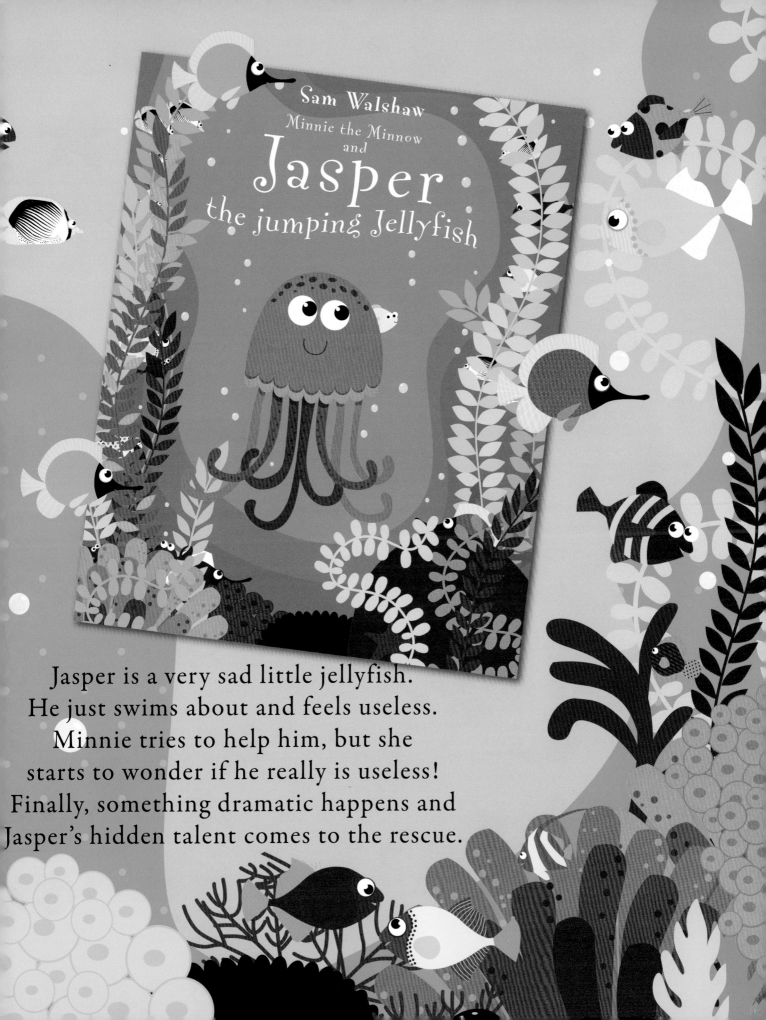

Sam Walshaw
Minnie the Minnow
and
Jasper
the jumping Jellyfish

Jasper is a very sad little jellyfish.
He just swims about and feels useless.
Minnie tries to help him, but she
starts to wonder if he really is useless!
Finally, something dramatic happens and
Jasper's hidden talent comes to the rescue.